]
M

**THE PROTECTOR**

"…the kind of intrigue I enjoy, much like Tom Clancy, Vince Flynn, David Baldacci, and Steig Larsen. In my opinion they have nothing on her."

*- Lt. Col. John Lund, U.S. Air Force, ret.*

**SHOW NO FEAR**

"If you enjoy good suspense, lots of action, plenty of plot twists and realistic romance, then Marliss Melton's *Show No Fear* is for you."

*- Novel Reviews, Book Reviews*

**TOO FAR GONE**

"Likeable and honorable characters who elicit sympathy and/or empathy."

*- RomRevToday.com*

**DON'T LET GO**

"4 Stars! Another winner in a top-notch series."

*- Romantic Times BOOKreviews Magazine*

**NEXT TO DIE**

"Melton brings her considerable knowledge about the military and intelligence world to this Navy SEAL series."

- *Freshfiction.com*

**TIME TO RUN**

"Melton…doesn't miss a beat in this involving story."

- *Publishers Weekly*

**IN THE DARK**

"Hooked me from the first page."

- *Lisa Jackson, NYT Bestselling Author*

**FORGET ME NOT**

"A wonderful book, touching all the right heartstrings. I highly recommend it!"

- *Heather Graham, NYT Bestselling Author*

**Novels by**

**MARLISS MELTON**

**THE TASKFORCE SERIES**

THE PROTECTOR (June 2011)

THE GUARDIAN (July 2012)

THE ENFORCER (Summer 2013)

**TEAM TWELVE NAVY SEALs SERIES**

FORGET ME NOT (Dec 2004)

IN THE DARK (June 2005)

TIME TO RUN (Feb 2006)

NEXT TO DIE (August 2007)

DON'T LET GO (April 2008)

TOO FAR GONE (Nov 2008)

SHOW NO FEAR (Sept 2009)

# LONG GONE

---

MARLISS MELTON

JAMES-YORK PRESS

©James-York Press, P. O. Box 141, Williamsburg, VA 23187

This book is a work of fiction. Any references to historical events, real people or real locales are used fictitiously. Other names characters, places, and incidents are products of the author's imagination, and any resemblance to actual events or locales or persons, living or dead, is entirely coincidental.



Published by James-York Press/July 2012
First Edition: July 2012/eBook
Second Edition: October 2012/paperback

For information about special discounts for bulk purchases, please contact James-York Press, P. O. Box 141, Williamsburg, VA 23187 or write to James-YorkPress@cox.net

Edited by Sydney Baily-Gould and Rachel Fontana

Book Cover Designed and Illustrated by: ©More Than Publicity
Interior Pages Illustrated by: ©More Than Publicity MoreThanPublicity.com
Interior Layout: www.formatting4U.com

Manufactured in the United States of America
10 9 8 7 6 5 4 3 2 1

ISBN-10: 1938732057 (digital)
ISBN-13: 978-1-938732-05-8 (digital)
ISBN: 10: 1938732065 (paperback)
ISBN-13: 978-1-938732-06-5 (paperback)

## FOREWORD

The characters and premise for this novella were born out of my Nov. 2008 release, TOO FAR GONE. At the end of that book Skyler and Drake were separated, their blossoming relationship cut off prematurely with Skyler's departure into witness protection. Readers have often asked me whatever happened to this couple. Read LONG GONE and you'll find out!

# LONG GONE

---

MARLISS MELTON

## ACKNOWLEDGMENTS

Any kind of publication, even a short one, takes a group effort. Many thanks to my co-author, Janie Hawkins, who helped—not just with this work—but with the whole second half of my Navy SEALs series. At last you get the credit you deserve, lady! Thanks, also, to Sydney Baily-Gould, my developmental and copy editor, and to Rachel Fontana, my associate editor for their time, insight, and devotion. I can't forget my loyal proofreaders, Marilyn Harper and Don Klein, or my cover artist at Wicked Smart Designs, Dar Albert. Still, this story wouldn't have been written at all if not for the support and enthusiasm of you, my readers. You've begged for years for Skyler and Drake's own happily-ever-after. Well, here you have it!

# Prologue

Stepping out of the employee elevator, Skyler hurried down the hotel corridor toward the housekeeping cart being pushed by her colleague, Jamila. The Sea Dip Hotel stood nearly empty on this weekday morning with scant guests visiting the ocean so late in the season.

At the sound of her approach, Jamila glanced back, slowing the cart to wait for her. "Caroline!" Her face reflected surprise. "What are you doin' here, girl? I thought you were off today."

"I was off," Sklyer conceded, catching her breath and tying the loose string on her apron. "But Nadia called this morning to say she wasn't feeling well, and she talked me into taking her shift."

"Shoot, she ain't sick." Jamila rolled her eyes. "You know she just drank too much last night, right? You shouldn't let her use you like that."

"I know, but I need the money."

Jamila ran an assessing gaze over Skyler's petite figure. "What's a classy girl like you doing workin' in a place like this, anyway? You should be sellin' time shares or somethin', not cleanin' up other people's messes."

"It's as good a job as any," Skyler insisted. "I don't need to be rich."

She'd been wealthy all of her life up until four years ago. When wealth came at the expense of other people's fortunes, it was an empty luxury. Her father, head of the Centurion mob headquartered in Savannah, Georgia, had taught her that bitter truth. Luckily for Skyler, she'd inherited not only her mother's decency but also Matilda's journals which detailed the crimes Skyler's father had committed. Those journals had been her only weapon against Owen Dulay, and she'd used them to send him to prison, where he'd poisoned himself with arsenic. Or rather one handsome FBI agent had used them.

"True, but it ain't no sin to use what God gave you," Jamila said with a pointed once-over. "With a face and body like that, you could snag a rich ol' man and never have to work another day again."

Skyler shook her head. "I like to work," she insisted. It made the time go by faster. Besides, her face and body were the last things she wanted anyone to take note of, lest she be recognized. Being in WITSEC, the U.S. Marshal's witness protection program, she had adopted a whole new identity and look, coloring her golden hair auburn and wearing it long instead of short. WITSEC told her where to live, and in places like Myrtle Beach, South Carolina, a menial job was the only one she could find with her degree in interior design.

In many ways, being in WITSEC was like having made a pact with the devil himself.

Skyler pulled the master card-key from her apron pocket and picked up a stack of freshly folded towels.

"I'll take this side," she offered, ignoring Jamila's shrug as she knocked on the door with the *Make Up Room* sign hanging on the doorknob. "Housekeeping."

As expected, the room was empty with the curtains flung open and sunlight streaming in. Throwing herself into the mindless task of stripping the bed, she realized she'd been cleaning rooms at this mid-price hotel for almost five months now. Little chance of her running into her father's entitled friends in a place like the Sea Dip, that was certain.

It beat her first job in Omaha, inspecting cans in a food processing plant. The best job she'd found so far had been in Portland working as a veterinarian's assistant, but she couldn't stay there, either. It was all WITSEC could do to stay one step ahead of the Centurions. While her testimony had put hundreds in jail, there were others who'd escaped imprisonment because her mother's journals proved insufficient evidence. It was those men who kept Skyler on the run.

*The wages of my father's sins are still being paid*, she reflected, using a razor blade to scrape purple bubblegum off the bathroom tiles.

The debt was a heavy one. Heavy and lonely.

Especially lonely.

## Chapter One

It was something she had yet to get used to—sitting at a public bus stop in a tourist town without fearing that she'd be recognized. Listening to Jamila jabber nonstop about the trials of raising teenage boys, Skyler leaned back against the wooden bench and forced herself to relax.

*No one here knows who I am*, she assured herself.

It was mid-afternoon on a weekday. Tourists streamed out of the hotels to enjoy the mild September weather and teenagers, already out of school, cruised the strip in their souped-up cars, windows lowered and music blasting. The sun was warm, the air blessedly cooler than it had been in August. Skyler tipped her head back, drew a deep breath, and closed her eyes. When she opened them again, she was looking straight into the eye of a high-powered, telephoto lens, aimed down at her from a hotel balcony across the street.

She sat up straight and looked around. What could the photographer possibly be taking pictures of but the ugly parking area and the bus stop where she sat? With a stab of suspicion, she peered back up at him. At her intent stare, he swiveled toward his room and disappeared.

Skyler's scalp prickled.

Why would he have taken pictures of the bus stop? To capture the lifestyle of the working class in Myrtle Beach? Or to positively identify her?

"Caroline? Hey, there!" Jamila's face swam into view. "You're looking all peaked, girl. You best not be gettin' that flu. You know your friend Nadia won't be working her sorry ass for you, not even if you were dyin'!"

"I know. I'm fine, I'm just…" *Scared. And probably paranoid.* But this was how it always started. Men she'd never seen before started taking an interest in her, following her around. It had happened twice before. When she'd caught one man filming her with his cell phone, she'd told WITSEC, and they'd moved her the very next day. Another time she'd been chased down a dark alley on her way home from work. That same night, WITSEC had made her pack a bag and they'd moved her clear across the country. "You're right. I'm really not feeling well."

"Don't breathe on me, honey, cause I don't have time to be sick." Jamila put a good foot between them on the bench.

Tears pressured Skyler's eyes. Jamila had been her first and only friend in Myrtle Beach. She'd taken her under her wing, made her feel welcome. The last thing Skyler wanted was to be ripped from her new home just when she was settling in. *This has to stop.*

A bus rolled up with a screech and a cloud of fumes.

"Jamila, I might not be here tomorrow," she announced, standing up and heading toward it.

"Hey, that's not your bus! Where're you goin'?" Jamila protested.

If she moved fast enough, maybe she wouldn't be followed. With a final wave at her friend, Skyler boarded the crowded transit. She found an empty seat near the rear and peered out of the window. Her pulse sped up as the man with the camera popped out on his balcony again, a cell phone plastered to his ear and his eyes fixed on the bus she'd boarded.

Digging in her purse for her own cell phone, Skyler dialed her case handler.

He answered on the first ring. "Higgins."

"Some man just took my picture while I was sitting at the bus stop," she whispered.

Higgins remained quiet for a moment. "You think he recognized you?" he asked on an odd note.

"I don't know."

"Are you being followed?" he asked. Now he sounded bored.

His lack of urgency made her blood boil. Having had to relocate twice, she had a right to worry, didn't she? Craning her neck, she peered out of the bus again. Any one of the cars behind it might be following her. "I don't know."

Higgins grunted. "Look, just go home and set your alarm. If anyone breaks in, enter your safe room immediately and call me from there."

WITSEC had installed a tiny room at the back of her closet. Reinforced with steel and padded with Kevlar, it was unbreachable. While the safe-room assured protection from immediate danger, it failed to banish the suspicion that the Centurions had found her yet again.

That wasn't supposed to happen. The tradeoff for giving up her old life was supposed to be a guarantee that she wouldn't have to live in constant fear.

"Fine." Putting an end to the call, Skyler gazed outside to get her bearings. Her stomach churned with uncertainty.

At the main terminal, she would have to switch busses to get on the one that actually went to her neighborhood. Apparently, it was up to her to lose whoever might be tailing her.

**

Shifting her head on the pillow, Skyler checked her clock. It was 2 A.M., and no one had attempted to kill her yet.

She would like to believe that was a good sign and that the man with the camera hadn't been singling her out, like the guy with the cell phone in Omaha or the man in the alley in Portland. Only, she couldn't convince herself that was true.

Feeling restless, she rolled out of bed and padded to her kitchen.

She'd made the best possible use of space in the tiny

bungalow she called home. The walls were a cheery yellow, the hardwood floors polished to a shine. If forced to move again, she would have to redecorate on another shoe-string budget. At least it kept her skills sharp. One day, she would use her degree to make a living. No more cleaning hotel rooms or inspecting cans on the assembly line or soothing panicked animals.

She heated a mug of water in the microwave. Steeping a bag of chamomile tea in it, she carried the mug into her living room to brood.

In the dark room that surrounded her, not a single memento held any personal significance. Even the afghan she wrapped around her only reminded her of one that her mother used to cherish. She hadn't been allowed to keep a single relic or photo, not of her mother, her friends, or even . . .

She tried squelching her memories, but they rushed into her mind like snow melting on the first sunny day in spring. A vision of Drake Donovan gazing down at her in the aftermath of their lovemaking made her heart clutch.

She would never forget the day she had stumbled on her mother's journals and realized their incriminating information could free her from her father's ruthlessness. Giddy with relief, she had invited Drake into her bedroom to initiate her first taste of freedom. At the time, she'd thought he was just a gardener, handsome, sweet, sexy. Half in love with him already, she'd had no idea he was an undercover agent for the FBI.

Falling in love with Drake had changed her life, but

not in the way that she'd hoped. Because her mother was stricken with Alzheimer's, Skyler was obliged to testify against her father's associates on Matilda's behalf, thus condemning herself to witness protection. How naïve she'd been to believe, even for a moment, that Drake could protect her! In their determination to quell her testimony, Centurions would have killed him, plus any member of his family they could lay their hands on. But Drake had known that was the case. He'd done his job, helped put a lot of bad men behind bars, and then grudgingly surrendered her to WITSEC, for her own safety and for his.

There wasn't any question she still loved him. But to expect him to wait for her was a pipe dream. After all this time—four years now—he had surely moved on with his life, found someone else to love.

The thought carved a deeper chasm in her heart.

Resolved to try and sleep again, Skyler plodded back to the kitchen with her empty cup.

She had just placed it in the sink when a flicker in the corner of her eye had her turning toward the moonlit window. The silhouette of a man leapt onto her lowered shade.

She startled back on a gasp, and the man disappeared.

Had she just imagined him? A scratching at her back door nixed that optimistic hope. Someone was attempting to break in! In the next instant, her home security system started to wail.

Recalling Higgins' advice, Skyler scuttled to her bedroom. She snatched up her purse and her charging cell phone and headed straight for her closet, feeling inside for the tiny button that triggered the door to her safe room. With a hiss and a glow of ultraviolet light, the door slid open.

She leapt into the four-by-six-foot space, hit another button, and sealed herself inside.

The supplies at her feet, the retractable latrine, and the mat all meant she could survive here for up to a week if she had to, but it wouldn't come to that. The alarm would bring the U.S. Marshals to her rescue in half an hour, at most.

Higgins had told her to call him right away. *Let him worry a bit,* she thought, resentment bubbling in her breast. *He should have taken immediate action to protect me.*

Through the ventilation shafts that tunneled under the house, she discerned a loud *smash.*

*What was that?* The alarm fell suddenly silent. Skyler put her ear to the steel wall and listened over her pounding heart. The muffled voices that reached her sounded like they were being spoken under water.

"She's not here," said a distorted male voice.

"You sure this is the right place?"

The first man said something about following her home.

*I knew I was followed.* Her heart beat faster.

"Look under the bed. She has to be here."

*They'll never find me.*

"Call that number you got from her friend. Let's see if her cell phone rings."

*What?* Jamila would never have given her number to a stranger—oh, yes, she would, if the man resembled Prince Charming. Oh, God, if Skyler's phone rang and the intruders heard it, they would know that she was still here. She quickly powered it off, shoving it deep into her purse. She put her ear back to the wall.

"You hear anything?"

"Nah. The bitch must've turned her phone off."

Sweat filmed Skyler's upper lip.

"So what do we do? We can't stick around. The alarm's gonna bring the feds."

"I guess we try again tomorrow. Don't touch anything on your way out."

As the voices grew fainter, Skyler sagged against the enclosure, her fear draining away. All she could hear now was her own shallow breathing.

Any minute now, the U.S. Marshals—possibly Higgins himself—would be here to whisk her away. *Again.* She couldn't stand this. They'd had their chance to keep her safe and they'd blown it. How could the mob have found her yet again?

The two last times, Higgins had blamed it on Skyler, who'd admitted to making phone calls she shouldn't have. But not this time. She hadn't called anyone from Myrtle Beach. So maybe *she* wasn't the problem; maybe there was a leak in WITSEC. Or maybe Higgins himself had betrayed her location.

Skyler swallowed hard. As her father used to say, every man had a price.

The bag of supplies contained a change of clothing, water bottles, trail mix, and a wad of cash—enough to get her through the next few days. Hefting it off the floor, she looped the strap of her purse over her head and released the lock.

The lights dimmed and the door swept open. As she stepped from her closet, headlights strafed the walls of her bedroom. That would be the hit men leaving or the U.S. Marshals coming to see why her alarm had gone off.

Either way, she wouldn't be around to find out.

"I'd like a room, please."

The motel clerk took Skyler's wad of cash with a thinning of his lips, but he kept his comments to himself.

She wore pink plaid pajamas and no shoes. She had lost her flip-flops running through someone's muddy back yard. Her face was flushed with exertion. Who knew what the man was thinking?

"Check out's at eleven," he intoned, handing her a room key.

"Thank you." She rode the elevator to the third floor, found her room, and went straight to the phone beside the king-sized bed. She hadn't realized when she'd fled her home that her plan involved Drake Donovan, but of course it did. He was the only soul she trusted; the only person capable of helping her now.

She dropped on the edge of the bed and pulled the phone closer.

The last time she'd seen Drake was when he'd stuck his head into the back of the U.S. Marshal's vehicle where she'd sat with her mother. "Only if it's life or death," he'd whispered, scribbling his number onto her palm, his brown eyes brimming with sorrow.

She'd memorized his number on the spot. Weeks later, she'd bought a prepaid phone card so she could place that life-or-death call if the need arose.

Desperation had tempted her to use it twice—once in Omaha the night her mother died and again in Portland on her twenty-sixth birthday. She'd admitted as much to Higgins who'd grilled her after Centurions had found her in both places.

*But I never even spoke*, she'd insisted.

*It doesn't matter. They're obviously still watching him. Do you want to put him in harm's way? Don't call him again.*

But Higgins had to be wrong. She'd never called Drake from Myrtle Beach, yet the mob had still managed to find her.

So maybe the Centurions weren't monitoring Drake's calls. God, she hoped not because she had to call him. She wouldn't last a week on her own.

With hands that shook, she tapped out the numbers on her calling card followed by his number. Her heart suspended its beat as she waited for his phone to ring.

Then it rang and rang.

Just as she was sure her call would go to voice mail, he picked up.

"Donovan. Hello?"

Four years of loneliness, fear, and regret strangled Skyler's voice box. Clutching the receiver with both hands, she pushed his name through her tight throat. "Drake."

His mattress creaked. "Don't hang up." He sounded suddenly wide awake. "Please don't hang up again, you hear me, babe?"

"I won't." How quickly he'd recognized her voice!

"Good, now tell me what's wrong."

Where to start? "C-centurions came for me again. This is the third time it's happened."

"What's the program doing about it?"

"Nothing. I ran away. They're not keeping me safe like they're supposed to."

"Where are you now?"

"In a motel room in—"

"Wait! Don't say it. All I need is the room number."

"Um…" It took her a moment to remember. "314."

"Got it. Don't go anywhere, babe. I'll be there as soon as I can."

"Wait, h-how will you find me?" Panic made her heart race. "When will you get here?" She was terrified of letting him go.

"Soon, sweetheart. Believe me, I could find you anywhere."

His answer assured her that there was no Mrs. Drake Donovan lying in bed next to him. *Thank God*. Drake was going to rescue her, just like he had four years ago when she'd been faced with an arranged marriage to her father's peer, Ashton Jameson.

"I'll be here," she whispered.

Her only answer was silence.

## Chapter Two

Drake forced himself to hang up. God knew he didn't want to. Skyler's voice was manna to his hungry heart, and she so clearly needed him, too.

But he couldn't risk the off-chance that the mob was listening to his calls—not that he could see how. His cell phone had been issued by the Federal Bureau of Investigation. Uncle Sam had deemed it secure and untraceable. On the other hand, his affection for Owen Dulay's daughter had been no secret to the mob four years ago. If Centurions thought Sky might contact him someday, they'd keep tabs on him for as long as it took.

He should never have given her his phone number. But the thought of being apart from her had been more than he could bear.

Luckily, she'd only called him a handful of times and, better still, she hadn't even spoken. The only way he'd even guessed she was the caller was by the aching silence that echoed his greeting. One call had been from Omaha, another from Portland, and the most recent from Myrtle Beach.

He checked his caller ID. She was still in Myrtle Beach. A special program on his cell phone pinpointed her coordinates.

He leapt out of bead, stripping as he stalked into his bathroom in the basement of his mother's house in Arlington, Virginia.

Skyler's words replayed in his head as he showered.

How could Centurions have found her in the first place, let alone three times? WITSEC had a flawless record. No one in their protection had ever been targeted—until now. Obviously, something was amiss with the program. Once he joined her down in Myrtle Beach, he'd assess the situation and decide what to do.

As he toweled off, he pondered the fastest way to reach her. Driving to Myrtle Beach would take about nine hours. A commercial flight, with all the hassles of airport security checks, would consume at least five. Skyler needed him *now.*

Damn it, he would have to ask his father for help. If Connor Donovan weren't his boss in the FBI's Undercover Division, Drake would have nothing to do with the man since he'd walked out on Drake's mom after twenty-seven years of marriage. But Connor had a pilot's license and he owned his own small plane.

Swallowing his pride, Drake dialed his father's number and set his cell phone on his dresser in speaker mode so he could finish dressing.

Connor answered on the second ring. "What happened?"

Clearly there had to be a calamity for Drake to call his father—sad, but so true.

"I need a favor." He strapped his gun holster to his

calf and reached for his jeans.

"What kind of favor?"

"I need you to fly me to Myrtle Beach tonight, right now. It's a matter of life and death," he added, stepping into his Levis.

"Whose death?"

"Mine." Considering his life wouldn't be worth living if anything happened to Sky, that wasn't an exaggeration.

His father breathed heavily on the other end.

"Yes or no? I don't have much time."

"Fine. I'll meet you at the airport in half an hour."

"Make that twenty minutes—please," Drake tacked on. In truth, he was taken aback by his father's cooperation.

Connor hung up on him.

Stowing his phone in his rear pocket, Drake turned toward his closet to pack a bag. Having no idea what he was up against, he tossed a hodgepodge of clothing into his black duffel, stuffing in a dozen spare clips for his Glock 36, just in case.

He fetched his shaving kit from the bathroom. In the process of zipping it shut, his gaze fell on the box of condoms he'd purchased months ago for the purpose of expunging Skyler Dulay from his heart and mind. Only he'd never used them.

If the fates were kind, maybe he would never have to.

Drake had to give the old man credit. He'd filed a

flight plan, fueled up, and completed a preflight check by the time Drake joined him in the cockpit of his Beechcraft Bonanza.

“Let’s go,” he said, urging his father to take off right away.

Luckily, the weather was crisp and clear with a full moon and a light tail wind blowing out of the north. It gave the two-seater added speed as they climbed into the night sky and banked south.

“Are you going to tell me what this is about?”

The question came one hour into the flight. Drake had hoped the audio on the headset he was wearing wasn’t working. Instead his father had waited until they were three thousand feet up in the air to interrogate him. Typical. Keeping his gaze fixed on the thin veil of moonlit clouds, Drake answered “Nope.”

“Does this have anything to do with your current assignment?”

Drake spent his weekdays down in Freeport, Bahamas, posing as a yacht salesman in an FBI-coordinated effort to curb drug smuggling out of the Caribbean and into the United States. “Nope,” he said again.

“Did you tell your mother anything?”

Drake whipped his head around. “I left her a note.” He fought to keep his resentment from bubbling up, but it boiled over suddenly. “That’s more consideration than you ever showed her—especially the last time you walked out.”

Connor sighed. "You have no idea what happened with me and your mother," he said tiredly.

"I don't need to know," Drake snarled.

"Son, if this is company business, you need to tell me what the hell is going on."

"Don't call me son. I stopped feeling like your son the day I took over your household responsibilities."

Connor shot him a scowl. "Stick to the subject."

"I am. Trust me, Dad, the less you know about this the better."

"So...plausible deniability," Connor concluded, using a term coined by the CIA during the Kennedy administration. "You think I'd lose my job if I knew," he guessed.

"Exactly."

Gnawing his lip in frustration, Connor went back to fiddling with his instruments.

Drake, in turn, studied the stars burning light years apart in the vast expanse before them. They made him think of star-crossed lovers, fated never to be together.

Screw fate. He was flying to Skyler now, and nothing in the universe could stop him.

An hour and a half later, the two-seater came to a standstill at Myrtle Beach International Airport.

As the single piston engine wound down, Drake set aside his headset and unbuckled his seat belt. He was now within minutes of Skyler's last known location. Dawn silvered the sky above the trees dripping with Spanish moss. It had been three hours since she'd contacted him. He hoped she'd been asleep all this time.

"Thanks for the ride," he grated. He unlatched the door and was stepping out onto the wing when a large hand clamped down on his shoulder.

As fast and strong as Drake was, he hadn't inherited his father's stature. He had no choice but to halt and look back at him. "What?"

"That's it? You're going to go off on your own? I thought you were smarter than that."

Considering the trouble Drake might be walking into, he knew he could use his father's help, but not when Connor offered it like that. Besides, the options running through his mind weren't exactly by-the-book. He didn't want to get his father in trouble if he chose to go vigilante.

"I guess I'm not," he countered. Yanking free of Connor's hold, he slammed the hatch behind him and leapt to the spongy ground with his duffle bag.

Jogging toward the bright lights of the General Aviation Terminal, he placed a call on his cell phone to Hertz Car Rental. His alias, Tom Keane the yacht salesman, would have a vehicle waiting by the time he reached the lot.

He figured his father would fly off in disgust shortly. After all, leaving was what Connor did best.

# Chapter Three

Skyler dozed in fitful spurts, waking periodically with her heart in her throat.

Had she dreamed someone was knocking on her motel door or was it real?

Groggy with sleep, she rolled out of bed and stumbled past her lit bathroom. Wiping a grain of sleepy dust from one eye, she went up on tiptoe to peer through the door's peephole.

The familiar sight of Drake wearing a hoodie made her heart leap with joy. He had dressed like that when pretending to be a teenager at the homeless shelter her father had used to launder his money. It was there that they'd met—her as a volunteer, him as a runaway in search of a new beginning. The hood was pulled up over his head, leaving his face in shadow, but she'd have recognized him anywhere.

With a dry mouth and fingers that could scarcely unlatch the safety chain, Skyler hauled the door open. *Drake!* Her cry of anticipation curtailed abruptly as the light from her bathroom hit his face. *No, not Drake*. She was letting in a total stranger.

She tried to back up, to slam the door on him, only the stranger was stronger. Forcing it open, he shoved his way inside and pinned her against the closet with his sturdy frame. A moist cloth came out of nowhere, covering her mouth and nose and stifling her screams.

Caustic fumes scalded Skyler's airways. She caught her breath and fought her captor's cruel grip, but he was stronger. In her panic, she saw two more strangers slip into the room, including the man who'd taken her picture yesterday. Ordering his accomplice to fetch her belongings, he watched with a smirk as her attacker subdued her.

Desperate for air, Skyler's lungs convulsed. Cloying vapor seared her throat, and darkness pooled at the edges of her eyes.

*How did these men even find me here?*

Anguish speared her as she felt her consciousness slipping. She'd come so close to seeing Drake again.

**

Drake pushed the elevator button for the third floor. Then he jabbed the close-door button until the elevator finally lurched upward. The adrenaline juggernauting through his system rocked him on his feet. Anxiety twisted his intestines.

He had dreamt of the moment when he and Sky would be reunited; every one of those dreams had been impossibly sweet—not like this. Foreboding robbed him of any pleasant anticipation.

For Centurions to have found her *three* times,

WITSEC had to have unintentionally leaked her location. If WITSEC couldn't keep her safe then who could?

*I can.*

He pictured them running away together to a place like Thailand, where his sister, a CIA case officer, was assigned. Imagine making love to Skyler whenever he pleased and watching her graceful interactions with the locals! On one hand, it sounded like paradise. On the other, could he bring himself to walk out on his obligations to his mother the way his father had?

The doors parted with a chime on the third floor. *This is it.*

With a deep breath, he marched out onto the landing and turned left toward 314. At the end of the hallway, two men were pushing through the emergency stairwell exit, and one of them was carrying a woman.

The unsettling sight broke Drake's stride.

The woman's hair was auburn hair, not gold like Skyler's, but she could have colored it. He couldn't see enough of her face before they stepped out of sight to make a positive ID, but he swore that her scent—a blend of gardenia and honeysuckle—still hung in the air. Given the way her head had lolled on the man's shoulder, she had to be passed out, cold.

*They'd gotten to her first!*

The realization had him pausing to retrieve his Glock 36 from under his pant leg. Then he pursued the pair, slipping stealthily through the fire door in their wake. Several levels below him he could hear footfalls and low-pitched voices. There were three of them, he realized, not just two.

Silencing his footfalls as much as possible, he flew down the steps in hot pursuit. But they were already on the ground floor, now, exiting the building.

As a loud *click* signaled their departure, Drake leapt recklessly down the remaining stairs. He couldn't let them get away. Christ, how would he ever forgive himself?

Barreling through the exit on the ground floor, he found himself in a parking lot gilded by a gray dawn. Less than thirty feet away, the man who'd been carrying Skyler had just unloaded her into the back of the van and was about to climb in himself.

"Hey!" Drake yelled.

The man swiveled to look at him, and Drake raised his weapon, stalking the van with determination. "FBI! Put your hands in the air and step away from the vehicle."

The man assessed the immediate area, saw no one else and, with a shout at the driver, dove into the cargo area and slammed the door shut. The engine roared and the van peeled away.

*Oh, hell no.* Aiming his weapon at the left rear tire, Drake fired. But in the gloom and with the van in motion, he missed. "Fuck!" His rental vehicle was parked near the front of the hotel. His odds of catching up with the van were slim, at best.

But then a second pistol barked, and the van wobbled, but it didn't stop. At a hampered pace, it continued to make its getaway.

Drake sprinted toward his rental, wondering who had helped him. He jumped into it, revved the engine and zipped out of his parking space, having parked tail-end-in.

As he scanned the horizon for the van's taillights, he spied a lone figure, back-dropped by a brightening sky and standing near the lot's exit.

His father. What the hell? Connor must have followed him and fired on the van after Drake missed his shot.

Too grateful to be angry, he slowed just enough to let his father in then took off before the passenger door was even shut.

"You want to tell me who we're after?" Connor demanded irritably.

*Not really*. But now that his father was involved, Drake couldn't bring himself to reject his help. He just hoped he didn't end up costing both of them their careers.

"Centurion scum," he said, keeping his gaze fixed on the dark shape of the van bumping up the four-lane highway several hundred yards ahead of them. A couple of cars and three stoplights kept them much farther back than Drake would have liked. "We can't lose them. They've got Skyler." His voice shook on the last sentence.

Out the corner of his eye, Drake assessed his father's rigid figure.

"Skyler Dulay?" Connor asked in an inscrutable voice. "Last I heard she was in WITSEC."

"She was. She called me earlier this morning, scared

out of her mind that she was being followed. She said it'd happened before and that WITSEC couldn't protect her anymore. That's obviously the case." It was his training that allowed Drake to speak as though his heart wasn't sitting frozen in his chest, ready to shatter if the worst were to happen to her.

Connor scraped a hand over his bristly jaw. "I wonder what happened," he muttered.

"That makes two of us, but I'm not going to let Skyler disappear in the meantime. Look," he added well aware that he was overstepping his jurisdiction by meddling in WITSEC's affairs, "I appreciate you helping me out back there, but it would probably be best for you if I let you out right here."

"And let you deal with these bastards by yourself?" Connor set his jaw. "I don't think so. They're heading toward the highway, by the way."

"I can see that." Gunning through a red light, Drake managed to avoid losing sight of the van completely as he swung down a ramp off Harrelson Blvd. onto Route 17. Gratitude toward his father sat like a fat pill in his throat—necessary for his health, but uncomfortable as hell.

"Hang back," his father advised. "Let's keep the element of surprise here."

Drake slowed his speed. It was no easy feat to avoid being seen on the scantily populated, six-lane highway. Hiding behind a semi-truck first then changing lanes to get behind a car, he held back as far as he dared to avoid being glimpsed through the van's side mirrors.

"I know how to do this, Dad," he mocked. "How long has it been since you've been on the streets?" He immediately reined in his tongue. Now wasn't the time to vent his bitterness, especially when his father was lending a helping hand.

Connor ignored his jibe. "I can't believe they're driving on a flat tire," he commented, as they passed a strip of tire lying on the road. "So, I assume you've got a plan?" he asked a minute later.

Drake tightened his grip on the steering wheel. As usual, he was making this up as he went along. "I just want to get her somewhere safe," he said.

"And you don't want to involve LE, right?"

Damn right he didn't. Local law enforcement would be out of their league and in the way. "The less people involved the better," Drake said.

"Okay, so I counted three of them. We should take them down now, while we know what we're dealing with."

"You want me to push them off the road?" Drake balked at the thought. "Skyler could get hurt. They could use her as a hostage."

"True." Connor crossed his arms and frowned. "Plus, I'd like to know where the hell they're headed."

"Next exit," Drake supplied, as the van gave every indication of exiting the highway.

He edged into the left lane, making it look like he planned to go straight. At the last second, he horsed across three lanes of traffic and up the ramp just in time to see the van lumber down a long, tree-lined road. The last of the tire was peeling away, and the rim sparked on asphalt.

Braking at the stop sign, Drake waited for the van to slip around a curve before accelerating after it.

By the time he got close enough to see it again, it was listing heavily and turning into a marina. Boats, big and small, had been pulled out of the water for maintenance, crowding a large graveled enclosure. The road dead-ended at a building next to a pier accommodating several more boats. This early in the morning the small mechanics operation hadn't opened its doors yet. Not a soul was in sight.

"Pull in over there." Connor pointed as Drake braked to avoid being seen.

Complying, he nosed the sedan in the shadow of a landed sailboat. "Why is there a marina this far inland?"

"We're next to the Intercoastal Waterway." Drake glanced at Connor for a split second. Clearly, his father as a pilot who'd studied hundreds of maps over the years had a better grasp of the terrain.

However, the realization that Centurions intended to take Skyler away by boat had Drake shaking off his seat belt and throwing open his door. He shot out of the car, desperate to stop the thugs from taking her anywhere. Instinct warned him that there wasn't a moment to lose. He could hear his father following closely behind, whispering for him to slow down, as he crouched his way through the trailered boats.

The van had backed right up to the pier, adjacent to a huge yacht. Weak sunlight buttered the yacht's sleek curves as it swayed gently at its moorings.

From their hiding spot, Drake and Connor watched as the tallest of the three goons carried Skyler from the van while his cronies went to work changing the flat tire.

Even unconscious, with her hair tinted auburn, she looked like an angel—an angel in pink, plaid pajamas. Drake's lungs expanded at the sight of her.

As they approached the yacht, a thick-set gentleman with receding hair stepped out from under the awning on the main deck. His casually chic clothing screamed money, as did his aristocratic accent when he spoke.

"There you are. Step aboard," he called out.

"Holy hell, is that who I think it is?" Connor's whispered words reflected astonishment.

Drake took a closer look, recognition exploding in his mind. "Ashton Jameson," he breathed, recalling that the man had once been Skyler's fiancé. Connor had worked like hell to implicate him in racketeering, but there'd been a frustrating scarcity of evidence.

Clearly Jameson wanted to punish Skyler for betraying him. The tall man carried his victim on board, and Jameson gloated down at her. "Bring her in," he said, turning toward the expansive-looking cabin. Drake's gut knotted as they disappeared behind sliding glass doors.

"What do you want to do?" Connor asked.

Drake eyed him in surprise. Was his father really

asking him to call the shots? "We wait for the three stooges to leave," he decided. "Then we go after her."

Connor nodded. "Okay."

Drake narrowed his eyes. "That's it? You're not going to pull rank or call in the U.S. Marshals?"

Connor avoided eye contact. "I don't think they'd get here in time, do you?"

Drake didn't want to think about Jameson's immediate plans. "No." He looked back at the yacht. Every muscle in his body spurred him to rescue Skyler *now*.

At last, the tall man reemerged, stuffing money into his rear pocket. Stepping off the yacht, he hurried back to his accomplices who were tightening the lug nuts on their spare. Drake counted the seconds until the van finally drove off.

As it disappeared, Jameson emerged from the cabin long enough to shout up at the pilot house. "Take us home, boys."

"Shit," Drake muttered as two lanky men in uniform sprang into view on the uppermost deck.

With an "Aye, aye, sir," they descended the myriad steps to prepare the yacht for launch. Jameson ducked back into the cabin, shutting the glass door behind him.

"Three against two," Connor muttered. "You know, if you maim or kill anyone, you can kiss your career good-bye."

Drake rolled his eyes in disgust. "We're not going to kill anyone. Just trust me and follow my lead."

With an overblown gesture, Connor signaled for Drake to lead the way.

Together they crossed the gravel yard toward the pier. The deckhands took note of their approach, glanced at each other, and stopped untying the yacht from its moorings.

"Morning," Drake called, stepping up to the *Julius Caesar* with outward confidence. *Of course, Jameson would give his boat such a pompous-ass name*. "I hope I'm not late."

The men frowned at him. "Late for what?" one of them demanded.

Drake shot him a look of feigned exasperation. "Mr. Jameson didn't tell you? Must have slipped his mind. I'm Tom Keane," he introduced himself, "with U.S.A. Yacht Sales." He fished a business card from his wallet. "He asked me to stop by this morning and appraise the value of his yacht." Traversing the gang plank he handed one of the deckhands his card. "He thinks he might trade this baby in for one of my newer models."

The older man looked at the younger. "Did the boss say anything to you about this?"

The youth shrugged. "No, Skipper, but he gets a new boat every year, don't he?"

"Yes, he does, and he buys them from me," Drake smoothly inserted. "I'm sure it just slipped his mind. He did say he was busy lately. How about I take a quick look around, then you can fetch Mr. Jameson when I'm ready to assess the cabin. I brought my mechanic with me." He jerked his thumb toward his father, who sent the men a nod.

"Why don't you show my mechanic the engine room," Drake suggested to the junior deckhand. "That way, I can get started up here and it'll go faster."

"I'll go get the boss," the older man decided, backing toward the cabin.

"Sure, if you don't mind disturbing him," Drake said easily. "He must be pretty distracted to have forgotten our appointment."

The skipper backtracked toward Drake and jerked his head at his underling. "Go ahead and show him. What do you wanna look at first?" he asked Drake.

"How about the pilot room? I'll start up there and work my way down," Drake suggested. "A boat's only as good as her engine and pilot rooms, wouldn't you say?"

The skipper didn't say anything. Gesturing for Drake to precede him to the upper decks, he remained a safe distance behind him until they reached the pilot room. There he went straight to the phone by the wheel and picked it up, turning his back to Drake for the first time. "What did you say your name was again?" Clearly, he'd changed his mind about alerting Jameson.

That was Drake's cue to bring the man to his knees. He did so with a well-executed chop to the neck.

Even then, the skipper put up a good fight, forcing Drake to render him unconscious with a sleeper hold. Once the man went limp, he bound his hands behind his back using the phone cord and gagged him with a rag.

That done, he hurried down the steps in search of his father, trying all the while not to dwell on what might be happening to Skyler, who'd been alone with Jameson all this time.

# Chapter Four

A throbbing pain brought Skyler's hand up to her temple. She cracked her eyes open only to squeeze them shut again as nausea rose up and the pounding intensified. *Dear God.* Why was she lying on her back in so much discomfort?

The memories came flooding back—how she had foolishly opened the door to a stranger, been overpowered, and forced to breathe chloroform vapors. She jerked upright, only to be yanked back by something biting into her right wrist.

Rolling her head upon a pillow, she peered up at the handcuff chaining her wrist to a brass headboard. Her eyes flew wide as she took in the odd dimensions of an unfamiliar bedroom. The built-in cabinetry and rounded window drove home the realization that she'd been stowed aboard a boat.

One of her father's favorite methods of disposing of problematic people was taking them out to sea—and never bringing them back.

Yanking on the handcuff, she tried desperately to slip her hand through, only the cuff had been cinched too tightly. She fell back onto the leopard-patterned coverlet, defeated.

There was no denying the truth. *They* had found her.

A barb of terror lanced her chest and nausea roiled in her again. With a moan of misery, she leaned over the edge of the bed just in time to keep from retching on herself.

She felt better with an empty stomach, but before she could gather her thoughts to devise a means of escape, footsteps sounded outside the door. The knob turned and the door swung inward. The familiar visage of the man stepping into the room brought a gasp of recognition to her lips as he shut and locked the door behind him.

*Ashton Jameson, her one-time fiancé and a dedicated Centurion.*

The blood drained from Skyler's face as he drew closer, smirking. Dressed in khaki shorts and a yellow Bermuda shirt, he looked like he might have been vacationing in the Gulf for the summer tan on his broad face.

"I see you're finally awake," he drawled in his Charleston, old-money accent as he surveyed her critically. Sniffing the air, he peered around the bed and spotted the stain on the rug. "My mother was right," he said with distaste. "Not only are you a bitch, you're not even housebroken." Laughing at his clever metaphor, he circled the bed to stand on the opposite side.

The terror she'd suffered moments before receded. While she knew that she was dealing with a monster, she *knew* this monster. Ashton might be cruel, but he was also lethargic and dull. At least with him, she stood some small chance of escaping.

A quick inventory of every object near at hand showed nothing she could use for a weapon. She would have to rely on herself, then. Grabbing the brass headboard, she pulled herself into a sitting position, every muscle in her body braced for his attack.

But rather than jump on her, he sat on the edge of the mattress, causing it to dip and her to roll toward him. He stretched out a hand. The moist pads of his fingers grazed her cheek as he slid them from her cheek to her left breast, squeezing it hard. Repulsed, she forced herself to hold his snake-like gaze. A show of fear would only goad him.

"All those weeks when you belonged to me," he muttered, breathing hard, "you kept your thighs together like a Vestal virgin. Turns out you were sleeping with your federal agent, weren't you?"

Reaching for the waistband of her pajama pants, he tried yanking them down over her hips, but Skyler resisted, and his efforts got him nowhere. "You can't stop me from taking what's rightfully mine," he threatened, leaning over her.

Seizing her chance, Skyler jabbed her free thumb into his right eye and jackknifed her legs at the same instant, making brutal contact with his groin. WITSEC's mandatory course in self-defense paid off. With a bellow of agony, Jameson reared back and toppled off the bed.

With grim satisfaction, she watched him curl into a ball on the floor, one hand over his groin, the other over his right eye. But her victory, she knew, was only temporary.

"You bitch!" he screamed. "You fucking bitch! I swear you'll regret that move."

As she waited for Jameson's inevitable recovery, remorse plunged through her. She and Drake had come so close to being reunited. So close. Now she would never again know the joy of feeling his arms around her.

**

Flying down the steps to the main deck, Drake drew up short to see his father leaning against the door to the engine room, catching his breath. His left eye was already beginning to blacken and his upper lip was cut and bleeding.

"So, I'm a little out of practice," Connor admitted, returning Drake's astonished stare with a belligerent look. "The kid was a martial arts expert."

"Uh-huh." Drake looked around. "What did you do with him?"

Connor held up a set of keys. "Locked him in the engine room." He gestured toward the sliding glass doors. "I can hear a struggle near the front of the boat," he added more gravely.

His words tore at Drake, causing him to wheel toward the glass doors, intent on getting to Skyler *now.*

His father leapt in front of him. "Slow down, there, hotshot. Your silver tongue might have gotten you this far, but Jameson is probably armed and not averse to killing us on sight. We need to catch him off guard."

"Luckily, he's not expecting us," Drake retorted. Retrieving his pistol, he checked to see that his clip was full. His muscles quivered with rage. "You might have to keep me from killing the SOB."

Connor produced his own pistol from under his shirttail. "That sounds like something I would say."

Drake narrowed his eyes at him. "Don't kid yourself. You and I are nothing alike."

Connor's smile faded. "You're probably right, son. Come on." He gestured toward the cabin's entrance. "Let's get Jameson."

**

Ashton was recovering faster than Skyler had bargained for. As he pushed himself off the floor, still huffing with pain, she twisted onto her knees to face the headboard. Though it was bolted to the wall and tugging on it wasn't going to free her, still, she had to try.

A glance over her shoulder showed him crawling closer. Blood dribbled down one side of his face. His right eye was a pulpy red mess; his left eye burned with hatred. *Oh, God.*

Gone was his intention to rape her—she could tell that at once. His next words confirmed it.

"Now you've asked for it. I was going to end this quickly and painlessly, but not now. Oh, no. I'm going to drag it out for days. You'll be begging for mercy by the time I'm through cutting you to pieces."

The words came as no surprise. She'd known of the mob's torturous techniques since she'd read her mother's journals. Her only hope was to lose consciousness early on and never wake up again.

He lunged suddenly, making a grab for her ankles, but a quick heel-strike to his face foiled that intention. The delicate bone in his nose cracked. Jameson howled in rage and lunged again. Manacling both ankles at once, he yanked her knees out from under her.

Skyler's temple plowed into the brass bar, so hard that her head rang. She willed oblivion to overtake her, but with a painful tug on her hair, Jameson kept her conscious.

His weight pressed her hard against the mattress. He fumbled for a moment in his pocket. The sound of a jackknife springing open made her blood freeze. "I think I'll feed your flesh to the sharks."

The cold bite of a blade against her ear made her blood roar. Squeezing her eyes shut, she envisioned Drake to give her courage.

A deafening crash had her eyes flying open. Ashton sprang off the bed, allowing her to crane her neck in time to see two men surge through the door that now listed on torn hinges. Pointing their guns at Ashton's heaving chest, they shouted, "FBI! Get down on the ground!"

*Thank God!* Boneless with relief, Skyler watched Ashton point his switchblade at her rescuers and back away, blubbering threats. The younger of the two men kicked the blade from his hand while the larger tackled Ashton to the floor, grappling him into submission in seconds.

Then the first man pivoted toward the bed.

"Skyler."

She blinked to clear her vision as he joined her on the mattress, his gaze skimming over her for evidence of harm.

"Drake?" She caught his face in her free hand so she could be certain. His features, faded from memory after four long years, were suddenly, dearly familiar. "Is it really you?"

"It's me, baby." His chocolate brown eyes reflected a tangle of emotions ranging from delight to fury upon finding her chained to the bed.

"Get off me!" Ashton roared on the floor. "You're dead! You're both dead!"

The man straddling him just pushed Ashton's bloodied face into the plush carpet to shut him up.

Skyler banished the two from her reality. In her universe, she and Drake were alone, sitting knee to knee, gazing deeply into each other's eyes. How long had she waited for this to happen? "I have to be dreaming." The suspicion that her mind was playing tricks on her made her groan in despair. After that blow to the head, it was all too possible.

"Shhh. It's me, baby. See?" He pressed her hand against his chest where his heart beat hard and fast beneath his soft shirt. "I'm really here. You're safe. No one's going to hurt you again."

She caught back a sob of joy. He was real!

"Dad," Drake called over his shoulder, snapping her out of her trance. "See if you can find the keys to these cuffs. Then you can put them on him."

*Dad?* Skyler regarded the other man in surprise. His hair, evidently once as black as Drake's, was shot with silver; his features were craggier, but there wasn't any question he and Drake were related. Searching Jameson's pockets, the older agent turned up a set of tiny keys. Within seconds, Skyler's hand was free.

"Where else are you hurt?" Drake asked, rubbing her tender wrist and tossing the cuffs down to his father.

She shook her head to signify that she was fine but sobs of relief got the better of her. Drake pulled her close, crooning words of comfort in her ear as Skyler burrowed against him, letting his never-forgotten scent anchor her in the reality that he was holding her, shielding her.

Still, nothing could block out the reality of his father hauling a resisting Ashton Jameson to his feet. "Let's go," he said to his son, "before any of his friends show up."

"Right." Drake looked down at her with real concern. "Can you walk, babe? Or do you need me to carry you."

Skyler dashed the wetness from her face. "I—I can walk. He didn't. . . " She choked on the words, unable to articulate them. Scooting to the edge of the bed she pushed shakily to her feet, refusing Drake's help.

"You did a good job messing up his eye," he said with a grin that faded as he caught sight of the swelling by her temple. "That's quite a goose egg. You sure you're okay?"

"I'm fine. Could you carry my purse and the other bag?" She was pleased to see them stashed in the corner of the room.

As he went to collect them, Skyler's gaze slid back to the bed. If not for Drake, she would have bled to death there, one pint at a time.

With Drake's steadying hand under her elbow, she made her way through the expansive cabin, across the glittering deck and the gang plank to the pier, where shock caught up to her, sapping the strength from her legs. Still, she started to take one shaky barefoot step onto the gravel.

As she stumbled, she heard Drake swear beneath his breath before sweeping her off her feet and into his arms. He carried her and all her belongings effortlessly across a lot filled with landed boats. Locking her arms around his neck, Skyler concentrated on breathing, on telling herself that she was safe. The steady sway of the man who held her soothed her frayed nerves and she fixed her gaze on the tan skin of his muscular neck where she wanted almost desperately to place a kiss. Ahead of them, she could hear Drake's father prodding Jameson, ordering him to pick up his pace.

At last, they stopped.

"What's the plan?" Drake asked his father as he set

Skyler on her feet. The ground felt cold and she started to shake again. He draped his arm around her slender shoulders.

"Police Station," the elder Donovan said shortly. "I'm taking Jameson in for questioning. Skyler doesn't have to make a statement, yet; I can vouch for her about the kidnapping. Just put her up front with you."

The realization that Ashton would be riding in the same car robbed Skyler of a portion of her relief.

"And then what?" Drake demanded. "I'm not going to turn her into WITSEC."

"We'll talk about that later, once she's rested. After you drop me off at the station, you can find a hotel and sit tight for a while."

*For a while*. Skyler balked at how temporary it all sounded. Without another word, Drake helped her into the front seat, plonking her purse on her lap and stowing her bag under her legs before he rounded the vehicle to slip behind the wheel.

His father pushed Ashton into the back seat and slid in beside him. As she glanced back at them, he caught her eye. "Connor Donovan," he said, with a nod. "Now that we've met, I can see why my son would risk his career for you."

"Hey," Drake snarled over his shoulder, "keep your comments to yourself."

Skyler sat back and stared sightlessly at her unfamiliar surroundings.

Drake cranked the engine, backed up the car, and

drove them out of the marina.

"I don't know what you've got in mind, son," Connor cautioned from the rear seat, "but Miss Dulay belongs in protective custody. You need to contact the U.S. Marshal's office and turn her over to them."

"Bullshit," Drake retorted with an angry glare in the mirror. "They had their chance to keep Sky safe and they blew it—three times. Like hell I'm going to trust them to protect her now." He gripped the steering wheel so hard that his knuckles turned white.

"If there's a problem in the program, you can trust them to fix it."

"Why the hell should I trust them when she almost fucking died!" Drake shouted.

Connor drew a harsh breath. "So—what?—you're going to give up your career for her?"

"If I have to, then, yes," Drake answered.

A weight fell abruptly onto Skyler's chest. *What have I done?* Not only had she put the man she loved at risk for Centurion retaliation, but apparently she'd unwittingly jeopardized his career by forcing him to do the job WITSEC was supposed to do.

She ought never to have called him in the first place.

## Chapter Five

"We're not going to be here long," Drake informed Skyler as they stepped into their motel room, just blocks from the police station. "Only long enough for you to freshen up and recover. And then we're going to take off," he promised, dropping their bags and turning to face her. "I'm going to take you far away from here—so far no Centurion or WITSEC agent is ever going to find you again."

She looked so battered standing before him, so jaded, her eyes rimmed with exhaustion, that it broke his heart.

"Are you sure you're okay?" he asked. He ran a light finger over her bruised forehead. "Maybe we should get you to a hospital."

"I'm fine. I just…"

"What, baby? What do you need? I'll get it for you."

"I'd like to shower."

"Sure." He bit back the words, *But hurry*. They didn't have much time if they were going to stay ahead of the game. As long as she took a quick shower, he could use that time to devise a plan for their disappearance.

With a whispered, "Thanks," she slipped into the bathroom and he heard the lock click.

Drake pulled a worn address book out of his duffel

bag. Normally, he accessed his contacts through his cell phone, but he'd dropped that into the back of a pickup truck parked at the gas station where he'd filled their tank en route to this motel. Obviously, the fastest way anyone could track him and Skyler was by his cell phone. This little book, on the other hand, couldn't betray them. He carried it around for emergencies only, since it listed the private numbers of support personnel at the Bureau. He thumbed through the pages. Who in Support could get him a passport for Skyler on the sly and lightning fast?

*Not that guy. Not him, either. Nope, not her.* The staff at the Bureau were all straight-laced, by-the-book types. With a hopeless sigh, he tossed the list of numbers back into his bag.

Okay, so leaving the country by air probably wasn't going to happen. He'd take her out by boat, then. *Of course*. His undercover status as a yacht salesman opened all kinds of doors for them. First he'd switch the plates out on his rental and then drive them down to Florida. From there, they'd hop on a yacht to the Bahamas and then board a freighter bound for South East Asia. Boy, would his sister Lucy be surprised when he showed up at her place in Phuket with Skyler in tow!

Pacing to the window, he searched the parking area for any sign of suspicious activity. Several early birds were up and leaving the motel but, otherwise, the parking lot stood quiet.

He heard the toilet flush. Then silence. Would it be fair to Skyler to ask her to hurry?

The bathroom door yawned open. “Drake?”

He rushed to her side. “Yes?” She had shed her pajama bottoms, leaving her in just her shirt and her panties. He fought to keep his eyes off her smooth thighs.

“Would you take a shower with me?”

His body thrummed with enthusiasm. “Er…” How the hell was he supposed to turn that down? “Baby, we need to get a move on.”

“Okay.” She stepped back, glanced into the mirror and grimaced. “I wish I could brush my teeth.”

Obviously, she didn’t get the need for haste, but it wouldn’t throw their plans off too much if they washed up first. “Wait one sec.”

He brought his shaving kit to the bathroom, squeezed a line of paste onto his toothbrush, and handed it to her. As she brushed her teeth, he anticipated learning every detail about her daily routine in the days to come. When she was done, he took the brush back and scoured his own teeth while she turned the shower on.

It wasn’t until she pulled off her pajama top exposing her pert, perfect breasts that it occurred to Drake that they might not be leaving the motel as quickly as he’d planned. The soft inviting light in Skyler’s eyes made him realize she had more in mind than just a quick shower. His heart started to thump a little faster. “Baby, I don’t know if we have time to—”

“Shhh.” She placed a finger on his lips, stepping close enough to brush her breasts against his chest. “I need you, Drake. I need you to show me that I’m still alive."

She couldn't have said anything more coercive than that. Lowering his head, he kissed her lush, wide lips with as much restraint as he could muster, but just the simple touch of their lips sent ripples of pleasure flowing to his extremities.

Still, he held himself in check, letting her be the first to open her mouth, to slide her minty-tasting tongue between his lips in search of his. Relishing her trust, he vowed he would banish the nightmare of the last six hours from her thoughts.

He stripped off his shirt in one fluid move, baring his chest. Skyler's eyes widened as she looked him over. "You've gotten so much bigger."

Her words made him feel like Superman. "I've spent a lot of time at the gym. It helped to pass the time."

A shadow moved across her face. "Every day without you felt like forever," she reflected.

"That's why we'll never be apart again," he swore, tackling the zipper on his jeans and shucking out of them. His pant leg got stuck on his holster. "Sorry." He stripped off the holster and lay the gun on the granite countertop.

"It makes me feel safe," she assured him.

Anxiety speared him briefly. What if the U.S. Marshals caught up to them and took Skyler back? Worse still, what if the mob managed to find them, even on the other side of the world?

The vision of Skyler sliding her panties off her hips and down her legs chased all thought from his mind.

"You're so beautiful," he whispered, denuding himself with less grace, but with obvious enthusiasm.

She pulled back the shower curtain, and a cloud of steam wafted toward them.

"Careful, it looks hot," he cautioned as she stepped under the spray.

"That's how I like it." She beckoned him to join her.

With a groan of bliss, he dove into the deluge and drew her slippery curves closer. She wrapped her arms around his waist, laid her head on his chest, and released a long, shuddering breath.

For the longest time, she didn't move.

"We okay, here?" he inquired, tipping her chin up. With a stab of dismay, he saw that she was weeping.

"Wash me," she requested.

Wordlessly, he reached for the bar of new soap and lathered the washcloth she had set within arm's reach. Beginning with her neck and shoulders, he filled the enclosure with the scent of lavender as he soaped her. "You're so lovely, Sky," he murmured, longing to comfort her. "Lovely and strong." His words made her lower lip tremble.

He realized she'd had no choice but to be strong. Neither one of them had had a choice.

But that was about to change—*after* he demonstrated how truly alive she was.

As he washed the undersides of her breasts, Skyler raised her arms in an unspoken invitation for him to touch her *everywhere*. Setting aside the cloth, he used his bare hands to cleanse her soft globes. Every pass of his thumb over her nipples made them tighter, firmer. She moaned, dropping her head back.

"Still good?" he asked, trying not to think of the time slipping away from them.

"Oh, yes."

Going down on one knee, he took the cloth again and soaped her feet and ankles, moving leisurely from arch to knee.

She watched through heavy-lidded eyes as he drew the washcloth ever higher. The steady ascent made her breathe faster, made her curve her fingers into his wet hair. When he ran the terrycloth through the golden curls at the apex of her thighs, her pelvis tipped toward his touch. She swayed against him, parting her legs in a subtle invitation. Dropping the washcloth again, he eased his fingers into the delicate folds of her cleft. "Like a flower," he marveled, tracing the slick petals until her thighs trembled.

"I want you, Drake." The words came rushing out of her. "I want you every minute of every day, forever."

He surged to his feet, gathered her against him and said roughly, "Then run away with me, Sky. I'll take you so far from here that no one will ever find us again. We'll live together the way that we were meant to."

Her eyes pooled with tears. "Make love to me first," she pleaded.

When Drake turned off the water and threw a towel around them, Skyler knew she'd won the bid to distract him. It wasn't that she didn't want to be swept far away by the man she loved. If anyone stood a chance of keeping her safe, it was Drake. But at what cost? He would have to leave everything behind—his career, his family, his reputation—all for her. Not to mention that hiding her from WITSEC was probably a crime.

He had to realize all that. Otherwise, he wouldn't have let her distract him so easily.

But there was still one thing he *could* give her—the memory of this moment. In the lonely months to come, she would savor every detail.

Droplets sprayed the tiled floor as he swung her out of the tub and briskly rubbed her down. Grabbing her hand, he pulled her into the bedroom, yanked the coverlet and sheets from the bed in one grand gesture, and sent the pillows flying. And then he tackled her onto the mattress, careful to protect her from the weight of his body as they fell in a tangle of limbs and laughter, huddling together for warmth.

"I could never get enough of you," he confessed, as their bodies aligned in a way that left them both breathless.

It would have to be enough for now. "I love you," she whispered as he found her slick opening. Wrapping her legs around his thighs, she welcomed his possession.

With restraint that made her love him all the more, he claimed her inch by gentle inch until he filled her utterly.

Just as in that magical moment in her bedroom four years ago, they fit together perfectly, like a hand in a glove. In some ways, they scarcely knew each other. In others, she knew him better than he knew himself—which was the reason she couldn't let him run off with her.

With Skyler emitting soft cries of pleasure, her body squeezing around him so tightly it put him into a mindless trance, Drake roused to awareness just enough to realize they were being careless. He went still. "We forgot protection. It's in my bag."

Her grip tightened. "Don't get up," she pleaded, holding him closely.

"You could get pregnant," he warned as she rocked against him, sending him closer to his climax.

"I know." Lifting her head, she deliberately caught his lips in a kiss so sweet it threatened the last of his self-control.

"And that would be okay with you?"

"Getting pregnant? Having your baby? Hell, yes."

Her mild swear word made him chuckle. She was full of surprises. He tried to be the voice of reason, which didn't work so well considering his presently limited cranial functioning.

"That wouldn't be fair to either of us, Sky. We're going to have to travel for the next month or so. I can't have you feeling sick on a freighter across the ocean."

A tear appeared at the corner of her eyes, sliding into the hair at her temple.

Drake stilled for a second time. "What's wrong? Talk to me, Sky."

Her eyes resembled sapphire pools. "I'm not leaving the country with you, Drake," she informed him with lament. "I'm not turning you into a fugitive."

Stunned, he pushed up on his hands to gaze down at her. "I'm not sending you back to WITSEC. Hell, no. We're making a break for it."

She just shook her head. "No. As much as I love you and wish we could be together, I refuse to cost you your career, Drake."

His eyes burned with frustration as his half-formed plans went up in smoke. "Damn my father for saying that to you!" he raged.

"I'm glad he did. It woke me up."

"It won't be like that, Sky. I can find another job. I swear, I can take care of you."

"I know you can, but you shouldn't have to. Just give me this moment, right now." She ran her fingers through his hair, pulling him back down against her. "Stay with me every second, for as long as you can."

If she wanted to believe he could just leave her to her fate, so be it. He'd find some way to keep her safe without surrendering her to WITSEC and even without her knowing, if need be.

"The only place I'm going right now," he whispered, "is to heaven and back—with you."

Slipping a hand between their joined bodies, he teased the pulsing center of her pleasure to spur her toward release.

"*Drake*." She raked her nails into his back, arching toward his touch. "Oh, yes!"

"I know, Sky." Hanging on to his self-control, he urged her to orgasm. "I'm right here with you. You're safe now. I've got you."

With a cry, she climaxed, sobbing into the crook of his neck. In the next moment, as her muscles milked him, he joined her, giving in to the overwhelming fervor of their passion. He drove into her warmth, feeling for the first time in four years as though he were finally complete, at peace.

With his breath still gusting, Drake cracked his eyes to find fresh tears on her face. His heart gave a throb of despair that their time was running out.

"That's just the first time," he promised, feeling himself stir again. "It isn't over yet."

Her eyes swept open. "It was perfect." Tears of repletion rimmed her eyelids. "Just like I remembered."

Warmth spread through Drake's body. *God, I love her.* If she thought he'd let WITSEC anywhere close to her again after they'd failed so miserably to protect her, she could think again. He had friends who could do a better job than the program.

Not only was his sister married to a Navy SEAL, but Skyler herself had nephews whose mother, Ellie, had fretted over Skyler's circumstances for years now, and she was also married to a Navy SEAL. Between Lucy's husband, Gus, and Ellie's Sean, one of them surely knew a warrior willing and able to keep Skyler hidden in some remote location until the rest of the Centurions frittered away or forgot about her.

Drake had their numbers in his address book. A surge of optimism lifted his spirits. He now felt like he and Sky had all the time in the world to make love.

Kissing her thoroughly, he gave himself another minute to recover. Like warm wax, she melted around him, pliant and willing and wanting him with such bottomless yearning that he swelled with renewed desire as he pumped inside her. They strained ever closer, mouths open and hungry, bodies taut and damp with sweat.

With every desperate plunge, Drake's muscles clenched tighter. Urgency battled his desire to make the encounter last forever, to hold onto the magic and never let it end.

Glimpsing her flushed, wanton expression from beneath his heavy lashes, he took pride in his self-control. But then Skyler caught him staring. Their heavy-lidded gazes locked, and the mutual lust reflected in each other's eyes was their undoing.

"Drake," she cried as they spiraled toward orgasm together.

Like a falling meteor, they crashed into the atmosphere and exploded into flame. Lungs stripped of oxygen, his nerves singed but sated, Drake collapsed onto

Skyler, with no strength left in his limbs whatsoever.

"My God," she breathed her heart still pounding beneath his heaving chest.

Kissing her tenderly under her ear, he rolled them both onto their sides to protect her from his dead weight. The towel they had brought from the bathroom lay within arm's reach. He dragged it over to wipe away the sticky moisture on her thighs. Tossing the towel onto the floor, he pulled the covers up over them.

Skyler cozied into the curve of his body, drew the pillow closer, and shut her eyes. "So tired," she whispered. He watched the lines of exhaustion on her face slowly fade as she relaxed toward sleep. "I love you, Drake."

"I love you, Sky." His own eyes felt like they had sand in them. How long would Connor interrogate Jameson? Probably for hours. Maybe he had time to catch a few winks himself. That way, he'd wake up refreshed and clear-headed, ready to take action on Skyler's behalf.

That was his last thought before his eyelids slammed shut.

A frightening dream jerked Skyler awake. For an awful second, she thought she was still on Jameson's yacht, trapped in his smothering grip, a hair's breadth from having her ear cut off.

But it was Drake's handsome visage that filled her eyes as she turned her head toward the man holding her.

His rumbling snore muted the frantic thud of her heart as she gazed at him, memorizing every angle of his face, the way his dark lashes fanned his strong cheekbones.

God, it hurt to love him the way she did! But it would hurt so much more to watch him give up everything for her sake.

Involving him at all had been a mistake.

She had to leave. To take responsibility for her own actions so that Drake would not be reprimanded because, God help her, she refused to ruin his life the way her own life had been ruined.

Lifting his arm off her hip, she eased away from him and rolled stealthily out of bed.

"Wher're you goin'?" he protested.

"To the bathroom," she lied. She stood over him, watching as he lapsed back into slumber, branding the image of his dark head upon the pillow into her memory.

Then she turned away, picked up her bag and purse, and went into the bathroom to dress. Her body and her mind felt equally numb. This was something she had to do, not something she wanted.

Stuffing her pajamas into her bag, she took one last look at her pale, tight-lipped reflection and turned off the light.

With stealth she had learned as a child to avoid her father's notice, she let herself out of the motel room, closing the heavy door without a sound behind her. As she coursed the motel corridor, she marveled that just yesterday, she'd been cleaning guest rooms like the maids up ahead, working their way toward Drake's *Do Not Disturb* sign. The past twenty-four hours felt like a week.

She left the motel via the side exit.

The instant she stepped outside into bright sunshine, vulnerability assailed her. *What do I do now?* Exactly what she ought to have done last night—head straight for the bus station and leave town.

Traffic whizzed by, disorienting her. All the restaurants, all the souvenir shops along this thoroughfare looked the same. Which way was the bus station? She took a wild guess and started up the sidewalk.

The sight of a police officer rolling up out of his cruiser half a block away broke her stride. At one time, Centurions had infiltrated every level in law enforcement, especially the local level. The officer appeared to be handing out parking tickets, but she couldn't take the chance that he might recognize her.

Sure enough, he stopped scribbling on his clipboard to eye her intently.

Panicked, Skyler stepped off the curb between two parked cars and darted across the four-lane street. She had nearly made it to the other side when a car sped up, nearly plowing into her. She stepped back to avoid being hit, and it braked directly in her path. Startled by the close call, it took her a second to recognize the face of the furious driver behind his dark sunglasses as he lowered the window and demanded, "What the hell are you doing out here?"

*Special Agent Higgins.* What were the odds of

running into him so suddenly?

"Get in the car," he said, jerking his head toward the door behind him.

She glanced at the passenger in the seat beside him, stunned to recognize Connor Donovan. Drake's father had obviously alerted the U.S. Marshals to her whereabouts. An awful sense of doom dropped over her as her gaze slid back to Higgins' inscrutable expression.

"No." She backed away, and a car horn blared in her ear, making her realize she was standing on the double yellow line in the center of a busy street.

"It's okay," Higgins was shouting. Connor Donovan climbed out of the passenger seat.

The light had turned green and cars were whizzing past her, forcing her to run past Connor in order to reach the safety of the sidewalk.

He proved to be faster than she was.

Caught up from behind, Skyler kicked and squirmed as he carried her back to the car. Passersby regarded them like she'd lost her mind.

"It's okay," he kept saying. "It's okay, Skyler. We're on your side. None of this was supposed to happen. You'll be safe now."

## Chapter Six

A brisk knock at the door startled Drake awake.

He sat straight up. The silence in the motel room turned the surface of his skin cold. “Sky?” He leapt out of bed heedless of his nakedness and peered into the dark bathroom on route to the door, his panic blooming.

*She was gone*. The brisk knocking came again. Snatching up a towel, he girded his hips and picked up his pistol.

“Who is it?” he demanded, edging toward the door.

“Your father. Open up.”

Impossible. How had his father found him when he had no cell phone that could be traced, unless… He hauled the door open and saw that his guess was right.

Skyler stood in the hallway, dressed in clothes he’d never seen and sandwiched between Connor and a man whose attire screamed U.S. Marshal—black suit, white shirt, black sunglasses.

“What the hell?” he exclaimed, taking in Skyler’s chagrined expression.

“I’m so sorry,” she said in a small voice. “I had to leave before I got you in over your head. I ran into your father and . . . and I had to tell him where you were.”

Drake leveled a glare at the freckle-faced, square

jawed man in the suit. "Let me guess," he sneered. "You must be Skyler's case handler."

The deputy marshal didn't even attempt to smile. "Special Agent Hank Higgins," he said.

Drake rounded on his father. "Why'd you bring this loser here?"

"Higgins and I have some explaining to do," Connor answered. "Put that gun away and step aside, son. That's an order."

Drake met Skyler's pleading gaze and, with a shudder of resentment, went into the bathroom to pull on his pants.

His mind raced as the threesome let themselves inside. He shook his head. He cursed himself for not sharing his thoughts with Skyler before she fell asleep about his plan to protect her from a distance. But now it was too late. She'd run into his father who'd brought Higgins with him, even after that man's negligence had nearly gotten Skyler killed. What was Connor thinking?

Stalking out of the bathroom still buttoning his shirt, he found all three of them waiting by the window.

"Let's all take a seat," Higgins suggested.

"Fine," Drake said. Reaching for Skyler, he tugged her down onto the edge of the bed beside him. "You okay?" he asked as she hugged his arm to her chest, her expression wreathed in apology.

"I'm fine," she said. "Just listen."

He divided a curious look between the two men. "Listen to what?"

Connor sat forward, his elbows on his knees. "The first thing you should know is that Higgins didn't intentionally hang Skyler out to dry. What happened last night was a sting operation gone bad. We set it up together to get the evidence I needed on my end."

Drake shook his head, baffled. "Evidence for what?"

Connor drew a deep breath. "I'm sure you've heard of the Culprit," he asked.

"Of course." Who hadn't? More than one broken Centurion had dropped the Culprit's name during interrogation, identifying him as a key figure in the mob and imbuing him with the godlike power to protect or destroy his own kind. But no one had ever identified him, and every attempt to flush him out had been unsuccessful.

"We've determined who he is," Connor announced.

"We?"

"Higgins and I," Connor clarified. "Plus some of our colleagues in the Undercover Division."

Drake blinked in confusion. "Don't I work for you? Why wasn't I kept informed of this?"

It was Higgins who answered this time. "Because we figured the Culprit might use you."

"What? How could he use me?" He paused as possibilities flooded his brain. "Who the fuck is the Culprit?"

"He's our boss," his father answered. "Deputy Director Bill Milton."

Drake was shocked into silence as goosebumps ridged his forearms.

Connor nodded. "Milton's uncle was a mobster, remember? That's what gave us the edge at the outset of our investigation. He knew how the mob operated and who was who, even though he claimed to have no more allegiance."

"Wait a minute. If he was still a Centurion, why the hell did he rat on them?"

"It wasn't a question of loyalty," Connor answered. "It was all about extortion. For those who could pay him, like Jameson, for instance, he offered his protection. Those who couldn't— he let them burn, safe in the knowledge that they couldn't identify him since he'd hidden his identity for decades."

"Jesus." Drake ran a hand through his hair. "But there still had to be a leak in WITSEC for him to find Skyler."

"There was no leak," Higgins assured him, "though we considered that a possibility until Skyler admitted she'd called you, once from Omaha and another time from Portland. Both times, Centurions showed up a short time later looking for her. The phone calls had clearly given her away."

"But I use a secure phone," Drake protested. "How is that possible?"

"Believe me, I had the same question. I went to your father with my suspicions, and he acknowledged that the only way it was possible was for someone inside the Bureau to be monitoring your calls."

Drake shivered. "Bill Milton," he guessed. "But

how?"

"Remember that mandatory software upgrade on your phone a few years back?" Connor answered. "Every field agent in the Bureau had to have it, allegedly for security purposes. That was Deputy Milton's doing. He uploaded software on your phone that allowed him to bug your calls—in fact any conversation you have within range of your phone, whether it's turned on or not could be monitored."

So when Skyler had called him from Oregon and Portland and more recently from the motel last night, Milton had seen exactly where the call was coming from. His goons, already in the area, had come straight over to grab her.

"I can't believe it." Drake shook his head. "What made you suspect Milton in the first place?"

"Think about it. Every time a key Centurion went to trial, there was insufficient evidence to convict. But we *had* the evidence." Connor slapped his palm. "And only Milton could have made it disappear before each trial. When Higgins came to me with the suspicion that someone was monitoring your calls, I knew it had to be someone on the inside, someone high up, like Milton. Together, we devised a plan to leverage evidence against him."

"A plan," Drake repeated as pieces of the puzzle fell together. "Wait a minute, you set up Skyler intentionally?"

"Yes." Higgins clasped his hands together. "We

called you several times from Myrtle Beach, using Skyler's calling card and hanging up the same way she had. If our theory was right, Centurions would show up looking for her. Sure enough, they did."

Drake glared at his father. "You knew all this when I called you for help," he accused "Why the hell didn't you tell me?"

Connor grimaced. "You had your phone with you the whole time, didn't you? I couldn't take the chance that Milton was listening in. He'd know I was on to him."

"Don't blame your father." Higgins jumped to Connor's defense. "It's my fault our plan took a wrong turn." Pulling off his sunglasses, he sent Skyler a remorseful look. "I should have told Skyler what we were up to. That way she would have stayed in the safe room like she was supposed to."

"Why didn't you?" Skyler demanded, her voice quavering.

Higgins grimaced. "I didn't want you to panic. I figured as long as you went straight into your safe room, you'd be fine and I'd explain everything when I came to collect you. My men and I were right outside the entire time." His hazel eyes swiveled toward Drake. "When the intruders went into her house, we bugged their van. The minute they left, I went inside to get Skyler from the safe room. But by the time I got there, she was gone. She must have slipped right past me."

Drake shook his head at the man's incompetence. "What if they'd grabbed her before she went into the closet? What if they shot and killed her on sight?"

Higgins broke eye contact. "That's why we built the safe room," he muttered. "So that wouldn't happen."

"How did bugging their van help?" Skyler wanted to know.

"It allowed our analysts to record the call they made reporting their failure to grab you. The voice on the other end of the call belonged to Bill Milton."

With much to think about, Drake rubbed Skyler's stiff back. At least the so-called leak in WITSEC proved non-existent. It was his cell phone that had been compromised, pointing Centurions to the cities from which Skyler had called him. Knowing that, he felt better about sending her back with Higgins

"Don't you ever use Sky as bait again," he warned the agent.

"Not going to happen," Higgins promised. "I promise you'll be safe from now on," he said to Skyler.

Connor pushed to his feet and started pacing. "Skyler said you tossed your cell phone into the back of a pickup truck?"

"That's right. One with out-of-state tags."

"Good. Then Milton never heard this conversation. All he knows is that you called me this morning and I flew you down here and together we freed Skyler and arrested Jameson. Jameson's arrest is bound to make him nervous, though. When Milton sees the writing on the wall, he'll try to flee the country."

"Do you have enough evidence to get him

indicted?"

Skyler's frightened question pulled a reassuring smile out of Connor. "Possibly," he conceded. "Jameson is squealing like a stuck pig, but he hasn't fingered Milton outright—if he even knows who he is. At least what he's told the interrogators lines up with the evidence we already have."

"Why did the Culprit give Skyler to Jameson, anyway?" Drake wondered out loud.

Connor shrugged. "It was an agreement they came up with, one that kept Milton's hands clean."

Drake felt his agitation rising. "How do you know Milton hasn't fled the country already?"

Connor patted his cell phone. "Because his wife hasn't called me yet."

Drake regarded his father in surprise. "His wife is in on this?"

"She's our lead witness." Connor's confident smirk faded. "Listen, I can't waste another minute down here. I need you to take me to the airfield."

In other words, it was time to relinquish Skyler to the U.S. Marshals. Drake tightened his hold on her, every cell in his body protesting.

"She'll be safe," Higgins promised.

Drake hit him with a level stare. "You'll answer to me if anything happens to her," he threatened.

Higgins inclined his head in acknowledgement.

"Let's give them a minute." Connor gestured for the U.S. Marshal to join him by the door.

Left alone, Skyler and Drake turned to face each other.

He tried swallowing around the lump in his throat. "This isn't what I wanted," he protested.

"I know." She raised her hands to his broad shoulders. "But it's better this way, Drake."

Possibly, but it was hard to convince himself of that.

"What we shared today will give me the strength to keep going—" Her voice broke. "—without you," she added, her tears overflowing suddenly.

He locked his hands over hers and slid them to rest over his heart. "Don't worry. I'll wait for you, Sky," he swore. "For as long as it takes."

"I love you!" she cried, throwing her arms around him.

He crushed her to him one last time. "I love you more."

"Time to go," Connor called from the door, his tone less abrupt than usual.

Closing his eyes to savor the memory, Drake pressed a final kiss on Skyler's lips.

Then he stood up, jammed his feet into his shoes, grabbed up his possessions and headed for the door. He did not look back.

After the Culprit was apprehended and incarcerated, the Centurions who remained would be exposed and prosecuted. Then Skyler would be free to live her life with him.

Drake had to believe that. It was the only thing that

kept him moving forward.

**

Bill Milton was in a pissy mood. He had spent his entire morning trying to rectify the mistakes of imbeciles. Was there no one else in this whole world capable of discretion and forethought? The idiocy of those he protected and those who worked for him now threatened his own future. It was everyone else's damn fault he was being forced to bail out earlier than planned.

*He* had done everything flawlessly.

Snatching up his suitcase from the taxi that had picked him up at the movie theater and brought him to Ronald Reagan International Airport, Milton waved off the porter who stepped off the curb to help him. With his jaw jumping, he stalked through the automatic doors into the airport lobby and headed straight toward security with his carry-on bag, having printed off his boarding pass at a net café earlier.

The airport was crammed with traveling business people. Bill hated airports. Having owned a private jet for a decade now, he had yet to encounter the post 9/11 security measures that plagued the average traveler. But flying out of the country on his private jet was what Connor Donovan expected him to do.

Oh, yes, with a little probing, he'd discovered that Donovan was on a mission to expose him. His involvement with the Skyler Dulay fiasco down in Myrtle

Beach last month was no coincidence. If Donovan caught word that his boss was leaving the country, he'd automatically assume he was taking his own jet. Hence, the necessary but distasteful use of public transportation.

He'd told his wife he was leaving on a business trip. Armed with a passport identifying him as a German-American named Hans Steuben and wearing a convincing disguise that he had donned in the bathroom of the cinema near his home, he was confident of his ability to leave the country undetected.

He hadn't become Deputy Director of the FBI by being stupid.

Stepping into line at Security, Bill double-checked his false mustache. As he bent over to unlace his shoes, he spared a thought for the life he was forced to leave behind. His fat, discontented wife could go to hell for all he cared. He would miss his dog and his fishing boat and the almost limitless power he'd enjoyed as the notorious Culprit.

He placed his carry-on luggage onto the conveyer belt. But, hell, he had enough money in his Swiss bank account, padded by desperate Centurions, to buy himself a pack of dogs and a fleet of ships, so why waste time being sentimental?

Fixing his eyes on the body scanner ahead of him, he shuffled forward in his socks.

He asked himself if he was leaving the country prematurely. Surely Donovan, despite his suspicions, had little by the way of evidence to indict him, except that

Ashton Jameson, who was being held without bond, was copping a plea and spilling everything he knew about the Culprit—not enough to name Milton outright, but enough to root a kernel of uneasiness in his mind.

Yes, it was best just to leave now, while the leaving was good.

Edging closer to the woman in front of him, Bill impelled her toward the full-body scanner before the TSA agent even waved her over.

Then he'd be next. Once through security, he'd be on his way to France and then to Switzerland, free to live out his days like a king.

A whispered conversation of two TSA workers was his first inkling that his plan was about to backfire. The larger of the two men raked the line of passengers with a narrow-eyed look while consulting a photo in his hand. Bill's skin shrank. His sixth sense told him they were looking for him.

Sensing a commotion behind him, Bill turned to see his nemesis, Connor Donovan, in the company of his son and a gaggle of rookies, all casing the line of passengers. His pulse spiked. What were they doing here? How could they have known that he was leaving town, when his wife was the only one he'd told.

Averting his gaze, he assumed a placid expression while counting on his disguise to get him through security.

"Next," called a TSA agent, and Bill looked up to see himself being waved into the X-ray machine.

"Put your feet on the shoe marks and hold your hands over your head," said the agent.

Bill suddenly remembered that his doctor had warned him to avoid all imaging technology in case the magnetic fields interfered with the proper functioning of his pacemaker. Should he say something? Right now, he couldn't afford to draw attention to himself.

With sweat beading on his brow, he stepped into the scanner, put his arms over his head and held his breath. His heart pumped unnaturally fast. Was it the imaging causing that to happen, or was it the fact that both Donovans were coming closer?

The TSA agent touched a hand to the radio on his ear as if listening to what the X-ray tech was telling him. "Sir, do you have an implant in your body?"

The question confirmed Bill's guess. "Pacemaker," he said shortly.

Out the corner of his eye, he saw the younger Donovan's head whip in his direction. "That's him!" the young man cried, pointing.

Bill's heart galloped. The younger Donovan, with his *tendre* for Skyler Dulay had made him such an easy target for manipulation, but perhaps he had underestimated the kid's instincts.

"Er, I'd prefer to be patted down," Bill informed the agent quickly. He tried stepping prematurely out of the machine.

"Not so fast," the TSA agent growled, blocking his path.

"FBI. Everyone step back!" In one slick move, the younger Donovan produced a pistol. The crowd shrieked and ducked as all six special agents descended on the full body scanner. The TSA agent locked a hand around Bill's elbow.

Connor Donovan stepped up to him, his green eyes mocking. "Director Milton, you're under arrest for the deliberate concealment of evidence pertaining to the crimes of the Centurion mob, for conspiracy to commit murder, and for extortion" he announced. "We're taking you into custody."

Bill feigned bafflement. "Who's Director Milton?" He caught the eye of the TSA agent. "May I take out my passport?" he pleaded.

The dark-skinned agent frowned and nodded. "Go ahead."

"Oh, come on," the younger Donovan scoffed. "He's the flipping head of the FBI Undercover Division. Of course he has a fake passport." He lunged at Bill's face, seized one corner of his false moustache and yanked it off. Some of the artificial skin smoothed over Bill's cheek went with it.

The crowd gasped in astonishment.

Drake Donovan pushed his face into Bill's. "I know it's you, you son of a bitch," he growled. "You told me about your pacemaker six months ago. But you can bet we'll fingerprint you in custody just to make sure. We'll even probe your ass looking for the arsenic you've probably hidden in it. There'll be no killing yourself to avoid prosecution like Owen Dulay did. Now, turn around so I can cuff you." He grabbed Bill and hauled him around.

"You're arresting an innocent bystander," Bill insisted, struggling to free himself. He wound up with his ear plastered to a conveyer belt, his legs kicked apart, and his wrists in cuffs.

With a rubber burn on his right cheek, he roared, "I'll have you fired for this, Donovan! You'll be sleeping on the streets, living on food stamps by the time I'm done with you!" To his chagrin, bystanders chuckled at his vociferations, which completely belied his earlier impersonation. He lapsed into silence as he was hauled to his feet and prodded forward, surrounded by a phalanx of special agents.

"We'll read you your rights on the way to jail," the elder Donovan taunted.

Meeting the man's cool green gaze, Bill Milton experienced his first taste of chagrin, followed by fear.

# Epilogue

Drake swung his black Acura ILX into his mother's driveway. As he neared the garage, the beams of his headlights glanced over a powder blue Honda. It was parked under the old basketball hoop where Lucy used to beat the snot out of him whenever they played a pick-up game. The color of the car made him think of Skyler's eyes.

Damn it, it was useless. No matter how hard he threw himself into his work, he couldn't get her off his mind for more than a minute at a time. How long could he live like this?

Thumbing the button that sent the garage door rumbling open, he parked alongside his mother's Buick and closed the garage behind him. He wondered briefly who his mother's guest could be. Lucy wouldn't be caught dead driving a car that frou-frou color, so he knew the car wasn't hers. Besides, she and Gus hadn't made any plans to visit home for Thanksgiving, as far as he knew.

His mother wasn't dating someone, was she?

Between his job that had kept him down in Freeport for weeks and the effort it took not to obsess over Skyler, he was too exhausted to notice what Karen Donovan was up to these days. He gave a mental shrug, unable to whip up his curiosity long enough to keep guessing.

God, he was tired. He wondered if, beyond the actual meal tomorrow, he could get away with sleeping rather than helping to entertain whoever their guest was.

Dragging his briefcase off the seat next to him, Drake trudged into the house with it. Thank God his assignment in Freeport was over. Every time he saw a yacht, he thought of Jameson and what that scumbag had tried to do.

The aromas of a basting turkey and pumpkin pie hit him in the face as he stepped into the kitchen. His mother, girded in a flour-sprinkled orange apron, turned with a smile on her face. “There you are, darling. You’re starting to remind me of your father, working so late.”

*Don’t ever compare me to him,* Drake started to say but since his father’s efforts had put Bill Milton behind bars for the rest of his sorry life and uncovered key evidence against several Centurion elite, it was hard for Drake to hold onto his resentment.

“Smells good,” he said, dropping a swift kiss on his mother’s cheek.

“I left dinner in the fridge for you,” she said. The smile hovering around her rosy lips snared Drake’s attention. It occurred to him that she looked nothing like she used to look when she was married to his father. She’d cut her dark hair into a short, sassy style that made her seem ten years younger. Zumba classes had toned her petite body so that she looked thirty-something instead of fifty-two. It had taken her almost three years to get over his father's abandonment, but by all appearances, she was better now, and that was all that mattered.

If his mother could move on with her life, then why couldn't he? Because he'd promised Sky that he'd wait for her forever, and it'd only been two months.

"Thanks. I'll go change first." He started to head for his basement apartment when he stopped to ask, "Whose car is that in the driveway, anyway?"

"*That* belongs to my new interior decorator." Karen's brown eyes sparkled. She bit her lower lip to keep herself from smiling.

Drake frowned in confusion. "*You* have an interior decorator?"

"I'm redoing the living room and kitchen," she announced with a wave of her hand. "Time for a new look, don't you think?"

"Right." Either his mother had completely moved on or she was going through a midlife crisis.

"I hope you don't mind," she added, "but my decorator will be moving in with us."

"Mom," he protested. "You don't need to rent out rooms." A sudden thought speared him. "Dad hasn't been shirking on his alimony, has he?"

"Oh, she's not renting a room from me," Karen assured him. "She'll be staying in the basement with you."

"What?" His mother wasn't making any sense.

There was only one bedroom in the basement, only

one bed, and she knew his devotion to Skyler. . . *Wait a minute*.

"How rude of me," she suddenly exclaimed, casting off her apron. "Of course, you'll want to meet her first." Grabbing his hand, she pulled him into the living area. "Sasha, dear. My son is home and wants to make your acquaintance."

A raven-haired woman stood at the picture window wielding a tape measure, her back to them. Drake's heart suspended its beat as his disbelieving gaze recognized the slim, graceful outline of her hips. The hair color was different, but when she turned to look at him, the heart-stopping curves of her face confirmed his hopeful guess. "Sky!"

Dropping her tape measure, she ran into his arms. They met in a crush of lips and chests and thighs.

"Drake," she breathed against his chin. He could feel her trembling in his embrace as he buried his nose in the hollow under her ear to inhale the scent of honeysuckle and gardenia.

"It's really you." He pulled back just far enough to feast his gaze on her. "What are you doing here?" He tightened his hold on her. "Are you in danger?"

She shook her glossy hair, as black as midnight, with eyebrows dyed to match. "I'm fine," she assured him. Her eyes sparkled with news she was clearly dying to tell. "I'm free. Higgins said your father took down all the key players that Milton was protecting. WITSEC will continue to monitor my safety, and I still have to live under an alias, but I get to live my own life now."

"You're serious." He couldn't believe his ears.

"Completely serious." She clutched him tighter in her excitement. "I've decided to use my degree in interior design. Your mother has looked at my ideas and she's given me my first big job." Uncertainty overtook her optimism. "I hope that's okay with you."

He tossed back his head and laughed. "Okay? Okay doesn't come close, babe." He blinked back the tears in his eyes. "This is a dream come true." Turning with her in his arms, he eyed his mother in wonder. "How long have you known?"

"Just a couple of days," she said with a shrug and a doting smile. "It was your father's idea, actually."

"My father's?" Stunned that Connor would do something as humane as help to reunite two lovebirds, Drake didn't know what else to say. He teased his new, secure cell phone from his pocket, unable to wipe the grin off his face as he looked at Skyler.

"Hey, Dad," he said as Connor picked up on the first ring. He met his mother's gaze and said, "Mom says this was your idea."

"Yeah, well, don't thank me yet," his father cautioned. "I'm sending you overseas as a precaution. Of course, she can go with you."

Drake had thought he'd be working at Headquarters for the next year. "To where?" he asked, dreading the answer.

"Somewhere in the Mediterranean. You'll be briefed

on Monday."

He heaved a sigh of relief. No wonder Skyler's hair had been dyed black; it would help her fit in better in that part of the world. "Skyler tells me you've nailed all of Milton's favorites."

"Yes, I have. And every one of them is looking at life in jail," Connor assured him. "I'll tell you all about it over supper tomorrow."

But tomorrow was Thanksgiving. "Wait…" Drake glanced at his mother in surprise, but she turned away just then, slipping back into the kitchen. "You're having Thanksgiving with us?"

"That's what your mother wants."

"Oh." He had no idea what this meant, but his parents were old enough to figure out their own lives. "Okay. See you then."

"Yep."

As he put his phone away and reached for Skyler, he couldn't fathom ever being estranged from her. But, love, he realized, had many different stages, and he couldn't wait to go through them all with her and for them to know each other the way his parents did.

"How are you feeling?" he asked her.

She drew a shaky breath and let it out again. "Like this is all a dream? I don't know, I've been so excited, so scared that I can't keep anything down." She laid a hand on her flat stomach.

Drake glanced down as a thought skewered his consciousness. But her waist looked as trim and narrow as it always did. *Nah, it couldn't be.*

Still, anything was possible as evidenced by the fact that she was suddenly in his life again. It was like a shooting star had landed in his lap.

He shook his head, marveling. "Wow. Thanksgiving might not be here until tomorrow, babe, but I've never been more thankful than I am right now."

Her wide smile mirrored his sentiment. "I love you," she said.

"I love you more."

He sealed his assertion with a kiss.

## COMING SOON FROM
# MARLISS MELTON

## THE ENFORCER, **Taskforce Series**
Book #3 (Summer 2013)

When the Taskforce suspects a militia in West Virginia is behind the bombing of federal buildings, Special Agent Tobias Burke goes undercover with his bomb-sniffing dog to incriminate the militia's leader. Toby is prepared to play the role of a disgruntled veteran and to seduce former Army Captain Dylan Connelly, if that's what it takes to prove her guilt. But fiery-haired Dylan is unlike any woman Toby has ever encountered. Determined, intelligent, and achingly vulnerable, she sparks a white-hot desire in Toby to posses her, body and soul. As the evidence against the militia stacks higher, Toby must choose between loyalty to his country and attempting to prove Dylan's innocence.

## DANGER CLOSE, A Navy SEAL Book (2014)

When Lt. Sam Sasseville rescues do-gooder Madison Scott from drug-infested Matamoros, Mexico, he expects never to see the lovely humanitarian aid worker again. Boy, is he mistaken. The woman appears in every God-forsaken hot spot to which Sam is deployed. Furious with her, Sam insists he has better things to do than rescue Madison's sweet ass every time the shit hits the fan. In the end, though, it is Madison who must rescue Sam from an enemy he has never before encountered.

# Meet the Author

Marliss Melton is the author of nine gripping romantic suspense novels, including a 7-book Navy SEALs series and continuing with The Taskforce Series. She relies on her experience as a military spouse and on her many contacts in the Spec Ops and Intelligence communities to pen heartfelt stories about America's elite warriors and fearless agency heroes.

Daughter of a U.S. foreign officer, Melton grew up in various countries overseas. She has taught English, Spanish, ESL, and Linguistics at the College of William and Mary, her alma mater.

She lives near Virginia Beach with her husband, young daughter, and four college-aged children.

You can find Marliss on Facebook, Twitter and Pinterest. Visit www.marlissmelton.com for more information.

CPSIA information can be obtained at www.ICGtesting.com
Printed in the USA
BVOW021650260213

314241BV00009B/106/P